CW00418804

Mary Louisa Stewart Molesworth

The Green Casket

Mary Louisa Stewart Molesworth

The Green Casket

1st Edition | ISBN: 978-3-75243-967-0

Place of Publication: Frankfurt am Main, Germany

Year of Publication: 2020

Outlook Verlag GmbH, Germany.

THE
GREEN CASKET
AND
OTHER STORIES

BY
MRS. MOLESWORTH

CHAPTER I.—RUTH'S START IN LIFE.

'Then good morning, Mrs. Perry. It all promises very nicely, I think. You may depend upon our taking good care of Ruth, and doing our best to train her well. Naylor takes great pride in her training. You will tell Ruth what I say, and impress upon her those two or three broad rules, and if she attends to those, it will be all right.'

Mrs. Perry courtesied—her best courtesy, you may be sure; for it was not every day she was honoured with an interview by so grand a personage as old Lady Melicent Bourne of the Tower House, at Hopley. She had known Lady Melicent all her life, for before she married, Mrs. Perry's own home had been at Hopley; but I hardly think this in any way lessened her awe of the great old lady—rather the opposite. And there had been no small excitement in the neat cottage beside the forge at Wharton, five miles from Hopley, when the postman brought a letter from my lady's own maid, own cousin to Mrs. Perry, the blacksmith's wife, to say that the place of under-housemaid was vacant at last, and Ruth was to be sent over to be seen by Lady Melicent herself. Ruth went, and was approved of, and came home with a message desiring her mother to go in her turn to the Tower House for a talk with her daughter's future mistress. For Lady Melicent was old-fashioned enough to take personal interest in her servants; even the younger ones were safe to be 'known all about' by her.

'And she said it that nicely, mother,' Ruth added eagerly, for she had returned full of admiration and enthusiasm about the sweet old lady. 'You are not to ill-convenience yourself; any morning saving Friday would do, she said, from eleven to twelve, and Cousin Ellen is to see that you stay to dinner. Her ladyship remembers you as well as can be; she thinks I favour you a bit, and she hopes as I'll favour you in my ways too. And so do I, I'm sure, dear mother.'

And on the child chattered, for a child she was—not yet sixteen—and the only sister among several brothers who had joined with their parents in taking 'choice care' of little Ruth. Yet she was not spoilt; her mother was too sensible to have allowed anything of that kind. Ruth was unselfish, well-meaning, and straightforward, though with some weak points which her sheltered life at home had scarcely yet tested fairly.

She was standing at the cottage door—'father' allowed no hanging about the forge or gossip with the neighbours—scarcely in sight herself, but eagerly looking out for her mother, when Mrs. Perry appeared, walking rather slowly up the hill which led from the little railway station. In a moment Ruth's hat was on, and she had flown to meet her mother.

'Yes, love,' said Mrs. Perry, in answer to the girl's breathless, half-unspoken inquiry. 'It's all right. You're to go on Thursday week. And a very lucky girl you are, take it all together. Eight pounds wages, to be raised to ten in a year if you stop on and do well, church and Sunday-school every Sunday, and now and then an evening service if Cousin Ellen can take you; pleasant work and not too much of it, and best of all, a real good kind lady for your mistress.'

'I don't see as how it could be nicer, and not so far from home neither,' said Ruth. 'Why do you say "take it all together," mother? I see no wrong side at all.'

Mrs. Perry smiled.

'There's that to most things in this world, I misdoubt me, Ruthie. But I'm rather tired, child. We'll have a talk when I've got my things off, and have rested a little. It's hot to-day, and I've been on my feet a good bit. Cousin Ellen, she would have me to see all there was to be seen—she took me round the fields and showed me the cows and the dairy and the poultry-yard and the gardens. It's a sweet place, though not large of course.'

'Lady Melicent's been there a good many years, hasn't she?' asked Ruth, as they slowly ascended the hill.

'Nigh upon twenty-five. Ever since her husband's death, when she had to leave Bourne Park. She had no son, only Miss Rosalind, who's now Mrs. Vyner; so the Park went to a cousin, and my lady took the Tower House, not caring to stay as a widow too near to where she had been so happy as a wife. I remember her coming—her and Miss Rosalind—as if it had been yesterday. I was a girl of fifteen. Well, here we are, and I shall be glad to sit me down, I can tell you, Ruth.'

'And there'll be a cup of tea for you in half a minute, mother. It's all ready. I set the kettle on when I heard the train whistling—and it's just on the boil now. There's some hot toast too. Father and the boys'll not be in for over an hour; we'll have nice time for our talk.'

She took her mother's shawl and bonnet and ran off with them, returning

3

with the good woman's slippers. Then she drew close to Mrs. Perry's arm-chair the little table on which she had already set out the tea-things, and stooped for the crisp slice of toast, which she began to butter. It was all done neatly and carefully—with even more care than usual, for Ruth was touched and grateful for all her mother was doing for her, and the coming event of her leaving home for the first time was casting a tender shadow over these little duties and services—a shadow which the girl hardly herself as yet understood.

'Now then, mother,' she went on, when Mrs. Perry's first cup of tea had somewhat refreshed her, 'tell me the rest. What is it you're not so sure I'll like at the Tower House?'

'Nay, child. I didn't say that. It's nothing to mind. My lady spoke most kind and sensible. There's just two or three rules she's strict about, I was to tell you, and talkin' of them'll explain other things. She will have those about her to speak the truth, first and foremost, and to be civil and respectful when they're found fault with; and if you meet with any accident, Ruth—breaking or spoiling anything in your charge, you're to up and tell it, straight away. These rules she will have attended to. Others, like about being up in time in the morning, and never going out without the housekeeper's leave, you'd find in every house. But I can see that my lady's very keen about truth-speaking and no underhand ways.'

'*Of course*,' said Ruth, with a little surprise. 'But so would any right-thinking lady be, mother.'

'I don't know as to that—there's many as don't care much so long as the work's well done, about how things go on that don't come under their own notice. But of course no lady likes things broke and not told of.'

'I'd never think of not telling, never, mother,' said Ruth, proudly. 'I'd be only too anxious to make it good too, out of my own money.'

'There's many times that's impossible,' said Mrs. Perry. 'But here comes in the difficulty you may find yourself in. You'll not be under Cousin Ellen, you see, child—Mrs. Mossop, as they call her at the Tower House—being as she's the lady's-maid, but it's Naylor, the head-housemaid, you must look to. She's a good-principled woman, so my lady says, and so Ellen says; but she's inclined to be jealous, and she has a very queer temper. You must try and not put her out, and if so be as you should do so ever—for nobody's perfect—you must bear it patient, and not go complaining to Ellen. Ellen couldn't stand it, she says so herself: it'd make such trouble, and my lady couldn't have it neither. So it won't be all roses, Ruthie, but still nothing so very bad after all. A little patience, and taking care to be quite straightforward, and you'll make

4

your way.'

Ruth looked grave.

'Do you mean, mother, that if I broke anything by accident I must tell Naylor and no one else? I'm sure I hope I shan't break anything; but if I did, I'd much rather tell Cousin Ellen, or even my lady herself. She seems that kind.'

'Well, but that's just what you mustn't do, my dear. It'd make ever such a deal of trouble. If there was anything very serious—but that I hope there never would be—you might better tell her ladyship than Ellen. It would never do to vex her, so kind as she is, and speakin' for you for the place and all—and it would never do to trouble Lady Melicent if you could possibly make shift without. You must just try and be very careful, Ruth, and don't go and get afraid of Naylor; she's a good woman at heart.'

'Yes,' said the girl, 'I'll do my best;' but she gave a little sigh nevertheless. There is no such thing as perfect happiness in this world, Ruth was beginning to find.

The next few days were full of bustle, rather pleasant bustle than otherwise. There were her 'things' to see to, one or two new dresses to get made, the choosing of which had been deferred till her prospects were certain, though Mrs. Perry was far too neat and methodical not to have the rest of her daughter's modest wardrobe in good order. There was the purchase of her box, and the presenting of different little gifts by her brothers and some of her school-fellows; there was the bidding goodbye to the neighbours, and the farewell tea-drinking in the vicarage nursery, where Ruth was a great favourite, and had sometimes spent a few days when extra help had been needed. Altogether the little maiden felt herself something of a heroine in her way, and though the tears were not *very* far off when the eventful Thursday came, she managed to keep them from falling, and to wave back a last goodbye to mother, with a smiling face, from the window of the third-class railway carriage as the train whizzed out of Wharton station.

She had hardly time to realise she was off before it pulled up again at Hopley. Ruth could almost have found it in her heart to wish she had been going a *little* farther away; it would have seemed rather grander! But here she was; and there was Cousin Ellen on the platform looking out for her, a vision which Ruth was by no means sorry to see, in spite of her valour.

'How good of you to come to meet me, Cousin Ellen!' said the girl gratefully, as she kissed her.

'I thought you'd be glad to have me,' said Mossop, as we must call her. She glanced round a little nervously as she spoke. The Tower House dog-cart was standing at the gate, and a young groom was directing the porter to lift up the box. He was scarcely within earshot, but Mossop lowered her voice. 'I just wanted to tell you, Ruth, love,' she said, 'you must call me Mrs. Mossop now as the others do. And I must not seem to favour you, you know—mother explained, didn't she?'

'Yes,' said Ruth, 'yes, cou——, Mrs. Mossop I mean. I'll be particular,' but her heart sank a little—it seemed so formal and strange. Mossop saw the look on her face.

'Don't look so frightened, dear,' she said. 'You'll get used to it all, soon. Only I wanted you to understand, so that you won't feel hurt if I treat you just as I would another in your place. Now jump in—that's right. Yes, thank you, Joseph, that's all,' and off they drove.

It was not quite strange to Ruth. She had been several times at Hopley, and once, as we have seen, to the Tower House. But places wear a different air when we know we have come to them 'for good,' and though all looked bright and pleasant that still summer afternoon, Ruth caught herself wondering if she would ever think Hopley as pretty as Wharton, or the newly-restored church, of which she caught a glimpse through the trees, as beautiful as the old, ivy-covered one 'at home.'

There was no question of seeing Lady Melicent that evening, but to Ruth the making acquaintance with her seven or eight fellow-servants was even more formidable. Naylor, a thin, grave-faced, middle-aged woman, shook hands with her civilly enough, and told Betsy the kitchenmaid to take her up to the bedroom they were to share together. Then came tea in the servants' hall, at which Mrs. Mossop was not present. But the others were kindly, and after it was over Naylor took her up-stairs and showed her what there was to do in the evening, adding that she had better get her box unpacked, so as to be ready to begin work regularly the next morning.

'And if there's anything you don't understand,' the upper-housemaid went on, 'be sure you ask me. Don't go on muddling for want of a word or two.'

'Thank you,' said Ruth. But she felt rather confused. The house seemed very large to her, and compared with the vicarage at Wharton, which had been hitherto her model of elegance and spaciousness, it was so. And being rambling and old-fashioned, it appeared to a stranger larger than it really was.

'The first thing you have to do of a morning is to sweep and dust my lady's "boudore,"' said Naylor, 'and the book-room at the end of the passage opening from it. Then you'll come to me in the drawing-room, and I'll show you what to do. But there's no need for you to touch the ornaments, neither in

6

the "boudore" nor the book-room. I do those myself, the last thing when the rooms are finished.'

'Yes, thank you,' said Ruth again.

'My lady is very particular about her china. She has some very rare, though the best is behind glass and under lock and key, I'm glad to say.'

Then she sent the girl off to her unpacking, which would not have taken her long had she not lost her way by wandering up a wrong stair, and having to come down again to the kitchen to ask for Betsy's guidance, which made all the servants laugh except Naylor, who looked rather sour. But she smoothed down again when Ruth reappeared in a quarter of an hour, armed with her little work-box, to announce that her things were all arranged, and she was ready to do any sewing required. Naylor soon found her some pillowcases in want of repair, and Ruth sat quietly at work till supper, for her, soon followed by bedtime.

And so her first evening passed, and if some tears fell on her Testament as she read her verses, they were not very many nor bitter.

'I'll do my best,' she thought, 'and it'll be nice to write home in a few days and tell dear mother and all, that I'm getting on well.'

CHAPTER II.—AN ACCIDENT AND A SCOLDING.

 The Tower House, as I have said, was rambling and old-fashioned. Lady Melicent's boudoir was a pretty, simply-furnished room on the first floor; a long passage with windows at one side led from this to what most people would have called the library, but for which my lady preferred the less imposing name of book-room. This book-room was in the square tower which gave its name to the house; it had a window on every side, and all the wall-space that was not window was covered with well-filled bookshelves. It had a second door besides the one out of the passage; this second door led on to another and narrower lobby from which a stair ran down to the back part of the house. So that when Ruth had finished her morning sweeping and dusting of these rooms, she did not need to pass through them again, but withdrew with her brushes and dusters down the back-stairs.

The ornaments of which Naylor had spoken were some delicate old china cups and saucers and teapots on the boudoir mantelpiece, and on one or two brackets in the corners. In the book-room there were fewer; only a handsome old timepiece above the fireplace and some punch-bowls and Indian vases on a side-table. It was all very interesting and wonderful to Ruth when she found herself installed in the boudoir for her cleaning the next morning. She took the greatest pains to do it thoroughly and neatly, and was careful to put back everything, even to my lady's paper-knife on her little table, exactly as she had found it.

Then, looking round with satisfaction, she turned to the passage leading to the book-room. The morning sun was streaming in brightly, for the windows were to the east, and as Ruth stepped along, her eyes fell with admiration on an old carved cabinet standing against the wall. It had glass doors, and was filled with delicate and costly china, principally figures, which Ruth admired more than cups and saucers. On the top of the cabinet, outside, were also some beautiful things. A box, or casket, especially attracted her; it was of bright green—malachite was the name of the stone, but that Ruth did not know—set in gold, and it gleamed brilliantly in the sunshine.

'My goodness!' thought the little housemaid, 'it is splendid. I never saw such a colour. But how dusty the top of the cabinet is! How I would like to lift all the things off—there's not so many—and dust it well; but I mustn't, I suppose. Naylor said none of the ornaments.'

So she only gave another admiring glance and hastened to the book-room, just finishing her work there in time to tidy herself a little for prayers.

Lady Melicent read these herself, and when they were over, she called back Naylor, who led Ruth forward.

'I am glad to see you, Ruth,' said the old lady with the smile that had so won her young handmaiden's heart. 'You will feel a little strange at first, but that will soon go off. Pay great attention to what Naylor tells you, and I have no doubt you will get on nicely.'

Then with a word or two of inquiry after her mother, she dismissed the eager blushing girl.

'A sweet girl and a good one, or I am much mistaken,' thought Lady Melicent, as she poured out her coffee. 'I am sure I shall be able to trust Flossie with her, and there will be some time before that for her to get used to the place, and for Naylor to judge of her.'

The next few days passed quickly. Ruth was fully occupied in learning her work, of which, though not too much, there was enough. It was only at night sometimes, if she happened to be lying awake after placid, good-natured Betsy was asleep, not to say snoring, that Ruth felt a little, 'a very little,' she said to herself, homesick. But it always passed off again by the next morning, and she wrote cheerfully to her mother. Of Cousin Ellen she saw little, but this she was prepared for. On Sundays, however, Mossop generally managed to have a little walk and talk with her young relative, and often got leave for Ruth to go with her to the evening service.

Ruth had been about three weeks at the Tower House when the first cloud appeared on her fair horizon. It happened thus. At eleven o'clock every morning a small basin of beef-tea was carried up to Lady Melicent in her boudoir. Mrs. Mossop always saw to this herself, and herself as a rule carried down the pretty china bowl with a cover and stand in which the soup was served. For this bowl was a favourite of the old lady's; it had been a present from her daughter. Now one day Lady Melicent had a slight cold, and as it was chilly and rainy, a fire was lighted by Naylor at her desire in the boudoir, early in the morning. It so happened that Mossop was unusually busy, and after having carried up the beef-tea, she did not return to the boudoir to fetch the empty basin. Later in the day Ruth met Naylor on the back-stairs.

'Oh dear,' said the housemaid, whose arms were filled with linen from the laundry, 'I do hope my lady's fire's all right. Run in, Ruth, there's a good girl, and see to it. My lady's down at luncheon in the dining-room.'

Off flew willing Ruth. Doubly willing on account of Naylor's graciousness. For it was not often the upper-housemaid was so amiable. She was only just in time to rescue the fire, but with a little skill and patience she got it to burn brightly, and getting up from her knees she turned to leave the room. As she did so, she caught sight of the china basin.

'Cousin Ellen has forgotten it,' she said to herself; 'I'll take it down.'

She reached forward to lift it, but she was a little embarrassed by the wood and coals she was carrying, and somehow—who ever can say exactly how such things happen?—her hand slipped, or the bowl slipped, or her foot slipped—anyway the china fell to the ground, and darting forward to pick it up, Ruth saw to her horror that the basin was broken into several pieces. The poor girl was sadly distressed. Still she did not think it so *very* bad, for she knew nothing of the history of the china. She gathered it together, and went slowly down-stairs in search of Naylor. She met her just at the kitchen door.

'O Naylor,' she said anxiously, 'I am so sorry. I've had an accident, and my lady's soup-bowl is broke.'

She held it out as she spoke; she was not afraid; she was just simply, as she said 'so sorry,' but quite unprepared for the storm that burst upon her. How Naylor did scold! Every sharp word she could think of was hurled at Ruth; strangest of all she was almost the *most* blamed for having done as she had been told, in at once and straight-forwardly telling what had occurred.

'Bold, impudent, and impertinent girl that you are, to come like that, as cool as a cucumber. "O Naylor, I've broke my lady's bowl,"' and here she imitated the girl's tone and voice in a very insulting way, 'as if you'd something pleasant to tell.'

Pale and trembling, Ruth stood endeavouring to keep back her tears. 'If I could match it,' she said, 'I'd do anything.'

'Match it!' said Naylor contemptuously. 'Why, Mrs. Vyner brought it herself from Paris, or somewhere farther off still. It's china as you never sees the likes of in a shop. *Match* it, indeed!'

'I didn't know'—— began the girl, but it was no use; her sobs and tears burst out, and she rushed away—up to her own room, nearly knocking down Mossop on the stair.

'Why, child, whatever's the?'—— she began; but Ruth only shook her head and flew on. She had been warned not to complain to Cousin Ellen, and she wasn't going to do so. She cried till her eyes were 'like boiled gooseberries,' and then, suddenly remembering where she was, and that she had her work to do, she tried to cure them by plunging her face into cold water, and with aching head and still more sorely aching heart, crept downstairs with her needlework to the corner of the servants' hall where she sat of an afternoon.

'If only I could run away! oh, if only I could run home!' she said to herself.

Betsy consoled her in her own way, which was not a very wise one, though kindly meant, when the two girls were alone in their room at night.

'*I* wouldn't take on like that for all the chinay bowls in the world,' she said. 'Things must get broken sometimes. Not but what you brought it on yourself by telling. I'd have left it there where it fell, and let them think the cat did it.'

'But, Betsy, I promised my lady and mother too, as I'd always tell if I had any accident,' wept Ruth.

'And what did my lady promise?' said Betsy. 'Leastways *I* was promised as I'd never be scolded if I up and told if I broke anything. Catch me! I'll not risk it. And if you'd any sense, you'd not trust their fine words no more than I do.'

'It wasn't my lady. I don't believe she'd scold. But Naylor is really *dreadful* when she loses her temper,' and Ruth shivered at the mere recollection.

'Then take my advice, and don't you tell on yourself never again, whatever happens.'

Ruth did not answer. She was tired out, and did not feel as if she could argue with Betsy. The next day things had calmed down again. Naylor was quiet and rather subdued, and nothing more, rather to Ruth's surprise, was said about the bowl. But the girl felt nervous and upset. It seemed to her as if it would be long before she got back the happy bright confidence she had been so full of.

But Ruth was very young; at her age troubles *do* melt away, however terrible they seem at the time. She had felt inclined at first to write off a long letter to her mother, telling her how miserable she was, and how she didn't think she *could* bear it. But a little reflection showed her that this would only make Mrs. Perry very dull and uneasy about her, and still more that if 'father or the boys' got hold of the letter—and it would, she knew, be rather hard for mother to keep it from them—they might insist on her being fetched home again, and there would be a nice ending to her first start in life! How everyone would laugh at her, and besides—would she not *deserve* to be laughed at, if she showed so little courage and patience? On the whole she decided to wait a bit, and in this I think she was right. It is a very different thing when a girl away from home conceals from her parents anything really *wrong*: Ruth had not done wrong; and indeed no one was much to blame for the trouble, except Naylor for losing her temper. And—and—after all, Ruth asked herself, would it be *quite* nice for her to write off a long description of the housemaid's infirmity, for a real infirmity it was? She did not want to lower Lady Melicent's household, and perhaps have Naylor gossiped about in the neighbourhood through her. For there was no saying how her indignant brothers might chatter. Anyway she would wait till she could have a talk with Cousin Ellen.

This came on Sunday. As Ruth was starting for the children's service in the afternoon, which she had been told she might always attend, as it only came once a month, she heard some one calling her, and standing still to see who it was, in another moment Mrs. Mossop appeared.

'O Cousin Ellen,' said Ruth joyfully, 'are you coming to church? I am so glad.'

'I thought maybe you'd like a walk and a talk with me,' said the lady's-maid. 'I've not seen you to speak to since Wednesday, and I thought it best not to seem to be seeking you. But I *was* sorry, child; sorry both for you and for the accident. You must be very careful, Ruth.'

'I was as sorry as sorry could be,' said the girl. 'Indeed I'd have done *anything* if I could have got another bowl. But—did you know how Naylor spoke to me, Cousin Ellen?' and Ruth hesitated a little. 'It was just awful.'

'I know how she is,' said Mossop, 'but it's no use thinking about it. I was just glad of one thing, and that was that you told at once.'

Ruth hardly seemed to feel this cheering.

'I could almost have wished I hadn't told,' she said. 'I don't know *what* I'll do if ever I have to tell anything again.'

'Don't say that, my dear,' said Mossop, eagerly. 'After all, Naylor isn't my lady, and it's her temper. You'll find it much worse in the end if you hid anything, believe me. Have you written to your mother about it?'

'No,' said Ruth, 'I thought I'd wait,' and she went on to explain her reasons. Mossop approved of them.

'Yes,' she said, 'wait a bit. Writing makes things seem so much worse. Telling is different. Maybe I'll be going over to Wharton some day, and I could tell your mother. You'll feel all right again soon, and it's to be hoped you'll have no more bad luck. I can't say but what I was very put out myself about that basin—real "Severs" it was. I suppose, to go to the roots of things, it was my fault for having left it about. I said so to my lady.'

'Oh dear, Cousin Ellen, I'm sure no one could ever think *you* to blame,' said Ruth. 'Indeed, indeed, I will try to be careful.'

Her tone was rather melancholy still. Mossop looked at her with a little smile.

'I'm much mistaken if you won't be hearing something in a day or two that'll cheer you up. But I mustn't tell you about it.'

And Ruth could not persuade her to say more.

CHAPTER III.—THE OLD CABINET IN THE PASSAGE.

 The very day that Ruth was crying about the broken basin, a conversation which concerned her, though she little knew it, was going on a good many miles away.

In a pretty room in a large country-house—a much larger and 'grander' house than the Towers, a lady, sweet and young, was lying on a sofa. In front of her stood a little girl—a pretty little creature of eight or nine. She had a bright expression usually, but just now she seemed uncomfortable and ill at ease. She fidgeted from one foot to the other, and frowned as she looked down, and her face was flushed.

'Tell me, Flossie,' said the lady. 'You're quite old enough to explain. Why don't you want to go to grandmamma's? I should feel so happy about you with her while I am away, and then papa and I will come to fetch you when I am quite strong again.'

'Mayn't I go with you, mamma?' said the child.

Mrs. Vyner shook her head.

'No, dear, it is impossible. You must either go to grandmamma's or stay here with Miss Kelly. And if you don't go to the Towers, I must tell grandmamma that you don't want to go.'

'No, no,' said Flossie, 'don't do that, mamma; I'll go, but please don't be long away. And please tell grandmamma that I'm too little to be always in her room. Mayn't I have a nursery, like at home?'

'I thought you loved being a great deal with grandmamma,' said Mrs. Vyner in a disappointed tone. 'I don't understand you, Flossie. However, you are to have a sort of nursery, and there is a very nice young servant there who is to take you out and amuse you. For I should be sorry to disappoint Miss Kelly of her holiday when she has had none for so long.'

Florentia's face brightened a little.

'I'll go into the boudoir as seldom as I can, and *never* along the passage to the book-room,' she murmured to herself, but her mother did not catch the words.

It was a week or so after this—fully a week, it may have been ten days, after Ruth's accident—that Lady Melicent sent for her one morning to speak to her. Ruth felt just a little frightened; surely nothing was going to be said about the basin *now*, so long after?

But the old lady's kind face reassured her.

'I sent for you, Ruth,' she said, 'to tell you that for a few weeks your work is going to be a little changed. Not disagreeably so, I hope. My little grand-daughter, Miss Vyner—Miss Flossie they generally call her—is coming to stay with me while her parents are abroad. Her nursery governess is to have a holiday, so we must take care of her ourselves. Mossop will superintend, but you, Ruth, will be with her altogether. You will dress her, and take her out and amuse her. I feel that I may have confidence in you, for you have been carefully brought up, and you have shown that you are obedient and straightforward. I was sorry for my bowl to be broken, and I hope in future you will be more careful, but I was very glad you told about it.'

Ruth flushed a little; partly with shame, for she did feel she had been careless, but more with pleasure. She was glad to have pleased Lady Melicent, and she was delighted to hear the news. To be under Cousin Ellen instead of Naylor was nice of itself, and to have the care of little Miss Flossie *would* be a treat!

'Thank you very much, my lady,' she said timidly. 'I will do my best, and indeed I will try to be more careful.'

She felt in such good spirits the next day or two, that she did not mind the *rather* grim looks she got from Naylor. Not that Naylor minded a little extra work to oblige my lady, but she felt sure Ruth would have her head turned once she was removed from *her* authority, even for a time.

A week, then a fortnight, passed. All was ready for the little visitor. Two days before her arrival Ruth was sweeping the passage leading to the book-room early one morning, when her glance again fell on the cabinet and its contents. It was a very sunny day, and the bright rays showed off as before the green casket, and revealed at the same time that the cabinet was very dusty indeed. Ruth drew near. To a very tidy, expert housemaid there is a sort of fascination in dust. Her fingers quivered.

'I'm *sure* Naylor often forgets that cabinet,' she said. 'She'd much better let me do it. And what's more, I will, just for this once.'

She lifted off carefully some of the ornaments, and placed them safely on the floor. Then she raised the green casket, admiring it as she did so, when, oh horror! The lid seemed in some extraordinary way to detach itself, and fell to

15

the ground with a sharp sound; and when the girl, trembling with fear, stooped to pick it up, she saw it was in two pieces; a corner, a good-sized corner, was broken off! For a moment or two, Ruth was really too appalled to move; then she looked at it closely. It was a neat fracture, by replacing it on the box, and 'standing' the whole on the cabinet again, the breakage did not show. Just then Ruth heard Naylor's voice; quick as thought she put back the two or three uninjured ornaments beside the casket as usual, and flew down the passage to the book-room, and there Naylor found her a few minutes later, quietly dusting. The temptation to conceal this new misfortune was too great, and Ruth yielded to it.

At first she only said to herself she would wait till the evening—Naylor was in a fussy humour, she could see. But evening came, and then next morning, and her courage grew ever fainter, till at last came the day Miss Flossie was expected, and *then* Ruth felt it was too late. She could not tell *now*, and have a scene like the last time, just as the little lady arrived. And evidently Naylor had not discovered the breakage, though the cabinet and the ornaments were carefully dusted. This puzzled Ruth a little; she could only suppose that the upper-housemaid dusted with her feather brush without moving the things about. And she tried to put the matter altogether out of her mind, though there were times—when she knelt to say her prayers, morning and evening, was the worst time—that she could not succeed in doing so, and more than one night she cried herself to sleep, crying more bitter tears than even the day Naylor had been so harsh and unkind. For *then* Ruth's conscience was clear. Ah, the difference that makes!

Florentia proved to be a quiet, easily-managed child. Indeed she was rather too quiet in the opinion of her grandmother and the old servants, who had known her much more lively.

'Are you quite well, darling?' asked Lady Melicent one day. 'I never hear you racing about and laughing as you did in the winter. Wouldn't you like a nice game of ball in the long passage? You could play with Ruth at the end near the book-room where there is no furniture.'

'No, thank you, Granny,' the little girl replied. 'I'd rather go out a walk with Ruth. I like best playing in the garden.'

'And you like Ruth, dear? She is kind to you, I am sure?'

'Yes, thank you, grandmamma. I like Ruth, and she likes playing in the garden best too.'

A sudden thought struck Lady Melicent. 'Flossie,' she said, 'will you run and fetch me the atlas which you will see lying on the side-table in the book-room. Your mother wants me to show you where they are now, on the map.'

16

Flossie hesitated. Lady Melicent and she were in the boudoir.

'In the book-room?' she repeated.

'Yes,' said her grandmother decidedly, 'in the book-room. Be quick, dear.'

Flossie went. But she was not quick, and when after some minutes she returned, she seemed rather out of breath.

'Why have you been so long? It doesn't take a minute to run down the passage,' said the old lady.

Flossie grew red.

'I went the other way,' she said. 'I don't like the passage. I went downstairs, and up the back-stairs.'

Her grandmother looked at her keenly.

'What a strange idea!' she said. 'Do you think there is an ogre in the passage?'

But Flossie did not laugh or even smile. And just then Ruth came to fetch her. Lady Melicent sighed when she was left alone. 'I wonder,' she thought, 'if I took Ruth into my confidence, if perhaps she might help to make Flossie tell. I can see the child will not be happy till she does, and I do not want to ask her. I should be so afraid of making her deny it. Ruth behaved so well about my beef-tea bowl, I am sure she has nothing underhand about her.'

And the old lady looked quite anxious and depressed.

Ruth and her little charge meanwhile were sauntering slowly up and down the garden. In spite of Flossie's saying that it amused her to 'play' in the garden, it did not look very like it. She seemed spiritless and dull, and Ruth too appeared to have lost her usual bright happy eagerness. Neither spoke for some time; at last Ruth half started, as it suddenly struck her that she was scarcely fulfilling her duty.

'Miss Flossie, dear,' she said, 'wouldn't you like a game? It's not warm today, and we're walking along so slowly. Shall I fetch your ball or your hoop? Or would you like to run races?'

'No, thank you; I'd rather just walk along,' said the child. Then after a moment's silence she went on. 'I don't like much being at the Tower House now. Do you like it, Ruth? Would you not rather be at your own home?'

Ruth hesitated.

'Yes, for some things I would,' she said. 'But I was very pleased to come here.'

'*Were* you?' said Flossie, rather incredulously. 'You don't look very happy. I thought so the first day. I wrote to mother that you had a kind face, but not a happy one.'

'*Did* you, Miss Flossie?' exclaimed Ruth, rather taken aback. 'Well, at home I was called the merriest of everybody, and, and—I've been merry here sometimes.'

'But you're not now, Ruth,' said Flossie gravely. Then she peered up into the little maid's face with her big gray eyes. 'I'll tell you what, Ruth,' she said, 'I believe you've something on your mind. It's very bad to have something on your mind. *I know about it,*' she went on mysteriously.

Ruth grew scarlet.

'You know about me having something on my mind, Miss Flossie,' she said. 'What do you mean?'

Flossie did not at once answer.

'I hate passing that way,' she murmured to herself. 'I shut my eyes tight not to see the cabi——. What are you staring at me like that for, Ruth?' she broke off suddenly, finding the girl's eyes fixed upon her. 'I only said it's very bad to have something on your mind, and so it is.'

Ruth by this time was as pale as she had been red.

'But what do you mean—how do you know, Miss Flossie? How do you know I have anything on my mind, and what were you saying about the old cabinet?'

'I was speaking to myself. You shouldn't listen,' said Flossie crossly. '*I've* something on my mind, but you needn't ask about it. You may be sorry for me, just as I'm sorry for you, but you needn't ask questions about what it is.'

'I—I wasn't asking questions,' said Ruth, more and more bewildered. 'I was only wondering why—what—what made you speak of the old cabinet in the passage? Did anyone—Naylor or anyone—say anything about it since you came, Miss Flossie?'

It was Flossie's turn to start.

'No,' she said, 'of course not. Nobody knows—oh, I wish I hadn't come here!' she suddenly broke off, 'and I wish you wouldn't speak of horrid things, Ruth. You weren't here in the winter; you couldn't know. And oh, I *am* so unhappy,' and throwing herself into Ruth's arms, the little girl burst into loud weeping.

CHAPTER IV.—A DOUBLE CONFESSION.

This was what was on little Flossie's mind, and on her grandmother's mind too, for that matter! It had happened several months ago, during the child's last visit to the Tower House.

One day Flossie had a cold. Not a very bad one, but enough to make her cross and uncomfortable. She was tired of reading, tired of her dolls, tired of everything, and it was a very woebegone-looking little girl that came to say good-night to grandmamma.

'I wish I'd something to amuse me,' she said dolefully. 'If my cold isn't better to-morrow and I can't go out, I don't know what to do all day.'

Lady Melicent considered.

'I'll tell you what, Flossie,' she said. 'You might make some bead-mats. That would amuse you. I have some very pretty beads in the green casket that stands on the old cabinet in the passage—at least I think they're there. I'll see to-morrow.'

Flossie jumped with pleasure.

'Oh, that would be nice, granny. Can't you look for them to-night? I might make a mat for mamma's birthday. Mayn't I go and look for them?'

'No, dear. The passage is cold, and besides that, the cabinet is too high for you to reach up to. You might pull over some of the heavy ornaments and hurt yourself. Wait till to-morrow, and I will find the beads for you. I won't forget.'

Flossie was sitting reading in the boudoir the next morning, when Lady Melicent came in with two or three little cardboard boxes in her hand. She looked at the child.

'Flossie,' she said quietly, 'here are the beads. I found them up-stairs in my work-box. They were not in the green casket.'

'Thank you, grandmamma,' said Flossie. But she scarcely looked up.

'Don't you care about making the mats now, Flossie?' said Lady Melicent. 'You seemed so pleased with the idea last night.'

'I would like to make a mat for mother very much,' said Flossie, getting up

19

and coming round to her grandmother.

But that was all she said, and two days after, the little girl left rather suddenly, as her father came over to fetch her and her cold was better. And ever since then there had been a little ache in grandmother's heart about Flossie. For that morning, when she went to look for the beads in the malachite casket, she had found it broken, and speaking of it to Naylor, the housemaid had thought it right to tell her that it was Miss Flossie's doing.

'I saw her climbing up on a chair, when I was in the book-room,' said Naylor. 'And I heard something fall. It was the green box. She put it back again in its place, but the lid was broke off the hinges, and one corner off. I'm very sorry, and I'm sure Miss Flossie was, for I heard her crying.' Flossie was a great favourite of Naylor's.

'I wish she had told me about it herself,' said the old lady with a sigh. 'But don't say anything about it, Naylor. She will forget about it probably for the time, but when she comes back again, I hope she will tell me.'

Flossie did not forget about it, though she tried to do so. But the broken casket was the mysterious 'something on her mind,' of which she had spoken to Ruth. And the remembrance of it was what had prevented her enjoying as usual the thought of a visit to the Tower House, and given her such a dislike to the long passage which had once been her favourite play-room.

You can now understand with what a strange mixture of feelings Ruth listened to Flossie's story. She soothed the poor little girl as well as she could, though feeling dreadfully ashamed when Flossie went on to blame herself bitterly.

'It was so naughty and mean of me not to tell granny,' she sobbed, 'for she's always so kind. And sometimes I've been afraid she'd think somebody else had broken it. Do you think granny has never found it out, Ruth?'

'I can't say, I'm sure, Miss Flossie,' said Ruth sadly. 'But it's clear there's only one thing to be done now, and that's for you to tell my lady yourself all about it.'

'I'll tell her when I go to have my good-night talk with her,' said Flossie. 'O Ruth, I'll *never* hide anything again.'

Her words were fervently echoed in Ruth's heart. She was on the point of confessing her own secret to the little girl, but a moment's reflection made her hesitate. No, she too must tell all to Lady Melicent herself, and it must be for her to judge if Flossie should be told.

'And if my lady thinks me not fit to be trusted any more, and I have to go home in disgrace, I must just bear it. It's my own fault,' thought Ruth.

It was a tearful but a happy little girl who came trotting up to be undressed and put to bed at the Tower House that evening.

'Granny has been so kind,' she said, 'and I am so glad I've told her. It was dreadful to have it on my mind, Ruth dear. And granny has been telling me how good you were about the basin, and I said to her it was you that said I must tell. And do you know, she *did* know I'd broken it, only she waited for me to tell myself. It's never been mended, but now she's going to send it to be done.'

Ruth sympathised in Flossie's joy, and the child was too happy to notice the girl's sadness. All Florentia said only made her own confession the more difficult.

'There is no real need for it,' said the tempter. 'No one can be blamed now. Indeed, it was not you who broke it after all.'

But Ruth had a conscience.

Late that evening there came a timid knock at my lady's door, and in answer to her 'come in,' a pale and trembling girl appeared.

'Ruth!' exclaimed the old lady in surprise. 'Is there anything wrong?'

'Oh no, my lady. Miss Flossie's in bed and asleep, quite happy. It's not about her. It's—it's—oh, my lady, it's about me. I—I broke, at least I didn't, but I thought I did, and that's just as bad. I thought I broke the green casket, and—and—I couldn't bear to tell—just as there'd been such trouble about the bowl, and—if I must go home, I'll not complain, my lady. I'—but here she broke down into sobs.

Lady Melicent stared at her in concern.

'You broke or thought you broke the green casket,' she said. 'Why, Flossie has just been telling me, what indeed I knew already—that *she* broke it,' and she looked at Ruth as if she half feared that the girl was dreaming.

'That was how I came to tell myself,' said Ruth. 'Miss Flossie has been so unhappy about it that at last she could bear it no longer, and this afternoon in the garden she told me. And then I felt that ashamed to think that I, more than twice her age, and knowing how wrong it was, had been hiding what I thought I'd done. It was last week—I knew I shouldn't touch the cabinet, but it looked so dusty one morning I felt somehow tempted to do it, and the green box, leastways the lid, slipped—of course I see now how it was. The hinges were loose, and it was broke already. But I *thought* I'd done it, and I couldn't bear to tell for fear your ladyship should think me really too bad, and just as

21

Miss Flossie was coming and all. So I waited, and then I got so as I couldn't tell. I wondered Naylor never noticed it. I wouldn't have let another be blamed for it. But when she didn't seem to have found it was broke, I thought I needn't. And now I'm quite ready to go home; it's only what I deserve.'

'No, Ruth, I should be very sorry for you to go home. I am very glad you have told me now. You did not tell Miss Flossie?'

'No, my lady. I thought it best to tell you first.'

'That was wise. I think there is no need for Miss Flossie to be told of it. She has had a lesson herself, and she respects you, Ruth. It may make you feel ashamed, but that you must bear. I should not like her to lose her feeling of looking up to you. And I am sure you will be even more anxious than before to teach her to be perfectly open and straightforward.'

Ruth could scarcely speak; her tears, though they were tears of relief and gratitude, nearly choked her.

'And,' continued my lady, going on speaking partly for the sake of giving the girl time to recover her composure, 'I do not think it will be necessary to tell Naylor, either.'

'Oh, thank you, my lady,' said Ruth fervently. And she could not help smiling a little, as she caught sight of Lady Melicent's face.

'As for Mossop,' added Lady Melicent, 'I will leave it to you. I daresay you will like to tell her when you have an opportunity, as you are away from your mother.'

'Yes, thank you, my lady,' said Ruth again. 'And indeed—I don't think you will ever have reason to regret your kindness.'

She could scarcely speak yet: the tears were still so near. But little Flossie was not the only person in the Tower House who fell asleep that night with a lightened heart and warm gratitude to the dear old lady.

The rest of Flossie's visit passed most cheerily, and Lady Melicent had not reason to complain that she no longer heard her little visitor's merry voice and laugh about the house. And a very unexpected event came to pass before the end of the summer, which greatly added to Ruth's happiness at Tower House. Naylor got married! Her husband was the gardener at a neighbouring house; a very meek and mild little man who gave in to her in everything, so it is to be hoped her temper improved. The new upper-housemaid was quite as good at 'training' as Naylor, and by no means so great at scolding, which, I think, no one regretted. And Lady Melicent lived long enough for Ruth herself in time to be promoted to what had once been Naylor's post, which she filled with honourable faithfulness till her dear mistress's death.

In the old lady's will she left 'to her faithful servant Ruth Perry, a casket of green malachite.' That was many years ago. The green casket has for long been the most valued ornament of the best room in Ruth's comfortable farmhouse, and her children, and grandchildren too, have all heard its story.

LEO'S POST-OFFICE.

'Oh dear!' said Leo's mother, 'there, I have run out of stamps again. And I don't like getting them from the servants. It is so apt to cause mistakes. It is really very stupid of me. Have you any, Marion?'

Marion was Leo's big sister. She was fifteen.

'I have one or two—yes, three,' Marion answered. 'Will that do, mamma?'

'It must do; oh yes, I think there are only three letters that really matter. I can't send for any so late. The servants are all busy; these letters can be put in the pillar-box just opposite. But I really must not let myself run out of stamps in this way.'

'Some days you have so many more letters than others. It must be difficult to know how many stamps you need,' said Marion, who thought mamma so perfect that she did not even like to hear her calling herself 'stupid' for running short of stamps.

'I wish we had a post-office in the house,' said Cynthia, the next sister. 'I did so want a postcard to send to Fletcher's to order my new piece of music, and when I was out I forgot to get any, though mamma said I might buy a whole packet. It's cheaper—for you get twelve for eightpence, and if you buy one at a time it's a penny each.'

'Or two for three-halfpence,' said Leo. 'That would make ninepence for twelve, not eightpence.'

'That's just like Leo,' said Cynthia; 'he's always counting about money and things like that. You're a regular little merchant, Leo.'

'Don't laugh at him,' said his mother. 'He is very careful and exact, and being careful and exact doesn't need to make anyone selfish or miserly. Leo has always money ready for birthdays and Christmas presents.'

Leo looked pleased, but he did not say anything; he was always rather a silent little boy. But later that same evening, when he knew that his mother would be alone, he came up to her quietly.

'Mamma,' he said, 'I want to ask you something. Would you mind letting me have a little money out of my packet?'

'What for, dear?' she asked.

Leo grew rather red.

'It was what you were saying about running out of stamps that put it in my head,' he said. 'And what Cynthia said too about my being like a merchant—I would like to be a merchant, mamma, if that means selling things. I'd awfully like to have a shop, but of course I can't—at least not a proper shop. But oh, mamma, I've been thinking if I might have a post-office,' and Leo's eyes gleamed with eagerness.

'A post-office, my dear boy!' said his mother, 'how *could* you have a post-office?'

'Oh, of course I don't mean a regular post-office. I couldn't have telegraphs, nor get people to post their letters in our letter-box. You wouldn't like it, would you, mamma?' he said gravely. 'But I just mean a post-office for selling stamps, and postcards, and perhaps newspaper wrappers. And wouldn't it be nice for you, mamma, always to be able to get stamps in a minute, however late it was—you'd never have to say you'd run out of them, then?'

THE LARGE ORDER

Mamma smiled.

'Yes, that would be very nice, certainly,' she said. 'But it wouldn't be much good to *you*, Leo, if you gave your trouble and lent your money for nothing? You should make some profit, even if it were only a halfpenny on a dozen stamps.'

'Or a penny on twelve postcards,' said Leo consideringly. 'I might buy a whole packet and sell them in ones or twos. That would be very nice. But even without that, I would so like to have a post-office, mamma. It would really be a help to you.'

So it was settled. Mamma gave Leo five shillings out of his 'packet,' which was a private savings-bank she kept for him, and Leo, as happy as a king, set off to the chemist's shop round the corner, which was the nearest post-office in the neighbourhood, and laid out the whole five shillings in penny stamps, halfpenny stamps, a packet of postcards, another of newspaper wrappers, a few twopence-halfpenny stamps, and two or three foreign postcards, just in case mamma were writing to France, or Germany, as she sometimes did. The chemist did look rather astonished at such extensive purchases, but he was very civil and obliging; and as he was a nice man, Leo felt glad he had gone to him instead of to the big post-office a quarter of a mile off.

'For he must gain something on as much as five shillings,' thought Leo.

Then he came home and began to make his arrangements. He had to consult his sisters about them, but they were very kind and very much interested, and were quite pleased that the post-office should be in the schoolroom, which of course was as much their room as Leo's.

There was a little old-fashioned cupboard or bookcase in the schoolroom, in which, above the enclosed part which had glass doors, were two little drawers not used for anything in particular. On these drawers Leo had set his heart. 'They would be just the thing,' he thought. And luckily Marion and Cynthia thought the same. So the drawers were cleared of such contents as they had, and Leo set to work.

In one drawer he arranged all his wares, as neatly as possible—using the lids of some old cardboard boxes as divisions. There were the penny stamps in one, the halfpenny ones in another, the wrappers and post-cards behind. And as of course Leo could not stand all day long at the post-office to wait for people coming to buy, he made the second drawer into his 'till.' In this he made divisions too, one for the money paid for stamps, another for that for postcards, and so on. Each division was marked accordingly, so that every morning or evening he could count up his sales, and see that all was right. Besides all this, he wrote out in his neatest, roundest writing a set of *rules* for 'Hertford Square Post-office,' as he called it, and to the card on which these rules were written he fastened a pencil by a long string, as he had seen done in real post-offices for telegrams, and a number of tiny little papers on which everybody who bought stamps was to mark down the number they had had, and to drop the little paper into the drawer.

And then with great triumph he summoned mamma and his sisters, and Miss Nesbitt, and nurse, and the butler, and in short everybody he could get hold of, to come and admire.

'It is really very neat and nice,' said mamma; and by way of 'handsel' or 'good-luck' to the new post-office, she immediately bought six stamps, for which she gave a whole penny extra, though Leo explained that of course he did not expect that *usually*.

'I hope your rules will be kept,' said Marion who had been reading them over. 'The principal one is about paying at once. Well, of course, that's a very good rule. It is so easy to forget to pay for such little things, if one doesn't do it at once. And then about the time of closing every evening.'

'At eight o'clock—when I go to bed,' Leo said. 'I shall come round then for the last time and shut up.'

'But,' said Cynthia, '*supposing* mamma wanted a stamp quite late at night. It might happen, you know, and that was to be the good of having a post-office in the house. And if you had locked them all up'——

'I can't lock them up,' said Leo; 'there's no key.'

'Well then,' said Marion, 'I think you should make a rule that if mamma wants anything after eight, she should be allowed to have it, or if any one else does, they might too, if they got her to sign one of the papers. Of course it wouldn't often happen, but just in case.'

'Very well,' Leo agreed; 'I'll add on that new rule,' and so he did.

All went well for some time. The stock, of stamps especially, was sold out several times in the course of the first week or two, and everybody paid regularly. Once or twice, it must be owned, Cynthia forgot to pay, and more than once or twice people forgot to mark down what they had taken. But Cynthia was always ready with her pennies as soon as Leo asked her, and except for this the money was all right. More than all right indeed, for one day a friend of his mother's made such big purchases that he was quite cleared out, and had to set off to the chemist's at once, and thanks to this and to other smaller profits, by the end of the first week he had gained threepence, and by the end of the second, twopence-halfpenny more.

So Leo began to think his post-office a great success.

But one morning he had a start.

He had left all quite correct the evening before; the money was right, and he knew exactly how many stamps he had left, when he had made his last round, as he called it, at bedtime; but this morning, though the money was the same, the stamps were not; three penny ones were gone.

One morning he had a start.

Leo counted them all over and over again, 'to be quite sure,' even though in his heart he had been quite sure from the first. Then he ran up-stairs to ask his mother if possibly she had taken them after he was in bed, and forgotten to mark them down. No, mamma had not had any. Leo began to look quite distressed.

'Don't worry about it,' said his mother. 'It's the first time anything has gone wrong. I will pay the threepence, dear. It has just been some mistake.'

Leo thanked her and ran off, determining to count more carefully than ever. And for two or three days all was right. Then again, one morning, it happened again that stamps were missing. Two penny and one halfpenny this time!

'Dear, dear,' thought Leo, 'I don't like this at all,' and again mamma was consulted. 'If this goes on,' he said, 'I must give it up.'

But mamma advised him to wait a little; perhaps some one would remember having taken them.

So Leo waited, though far from easy in his mind. Only one thing consoled him.

'If it was a robber,' he thought, 'they'd have been *more* likely to take the pennies than the stamps.'

'IT REALLY IS VERY QUEER'

For some days poor Leo was in great trouble about the strange disappearance of his stamps. He asked everybody, but nobody had had any they had not paid for. And he was sure nobody in the house would say what was not true. He began to think of robbers and burglars, only, as Benjamin the footman reminded him, 'It wasn't common-sense to suppose burglars'd steal postage-stamps and nought else; not that there was much chance of silver plate about. Mr. Trev, the butler, and he—Benjamin himself—was a deal too sharp.'

Benjamin seemed a little cross about the stamps, and so did Trev, Leo thought. And mamma advised him to say no more about it. If it happened again—well, she began to be afraid he would have to give up his post-office, and for some evenings, to make quite sure, she counted them over herself with him at bedtime, and as they each time proved right the next morning, she almost thought Leo must have miscounted.

But alas! Two mornings after that, and again stamps were missing, two this time, and, by way of variety this time, a newspaper wrapper!

'It really is very queer,' said Leo's mother when he flew to tell her of the new troubles. 'I really do feel as if I would like to find out who takes them. I've a great mind to sit up late one evening and watch.'

'Oh no, mamma, please don't,' said poor Leo, looking quite frightened; 'at least if you do, you must let me sit up too. Just think if it was real robbers,' for he could not quite get the idea out of his head that burglars after all might have to do with it.

Mamma laughed, but still she promised him that she would choose a night when his father was at home.

'I don't think I should care to sit up late all alone,' she said, 'even though I don't think it likely that burglars are stealing your stamps, Leo.'

Now I must explain that Leo's father was a *very* busy man. Some evenings he did not get home till long after not only Leo, but his big sisters and even his mother, were in bed, and sometimes he had to go off so early in the morning that for several days together, now and then, they scarcely saw him. This was a great trouble to them all, for they were very fond indeed of their father, and he was very fond of them. But it could not be helped for the present, though Leo was already looking forward to the time when he should 'be a man,' and able to help papa.

Lately, since Leo had started his post-office, his father had been even extra busy, and if he had heard about the matter at all, he had not paid much attention, or else he had quite forgotten it. The schoolroom in these children's house was at the end of the hall, and between it and the dining-room was a tiny little book-room or study, where their father kept all his own papers, and where he used to write when he *was* at home. Sometimes when he came home very late and let himself in with his latchkey, he would go straight to this little room, where a good fire was kept up, and there he would write answers to any letters he found waiting for him, and leave them on the hall-table all ready to be posted the *very* first thing in the morning by whichever of the servants was the earliest about; but I don't think any of the children or their mother knew of this custom of his, as it had never happened to come in their way.

The very evening of the day on which Leo and his mother had been talking so seriously about the missing stamps, papa, for a wonder, came home quite early. It was really a great treat to them all. He had dinner quite comfortably with mamma, and after dinner, when Marion and Cynthia and Leo were all in the drawing-room as usual, they kept saying to each other *how* nice it was to have papa with them.

'If only you could come home every day as early as this,' said Cynthia to him.

'But perhaps if I could, you wouldn't think so much of me,' said her father laughing.

'And I'm afraid mamma wouldn't let me sit up till nine *every* night,' said Leo, who had got an hour's grace this evening. 'Mamma,' he went on, coming close to her and whispering, 'do you think you'll sit up to-night and *watch*? I wouldn't mind you doing it with papa, you know.'

'I'll see about it,' said his mother, smiling, while his father looked up and asked what they were whispering about—it was a shame to have secrets from him when he was so seldom at home!

And as he spoke, he got up slowly from his comfortable chair by the fire.

'I'm afraid I must go down-stairs to the study,' he said. 'I have some letters to write, though I do feel very lazy about it.'

But immediately a cry was set up.

'O papa, do wait till we've gone to bed,' said the three voices. 'We shall be going in half an hour.'

So of course papa gave in.

Mamma had an interesting book to read after the children had gone to bed, and their father had left her to write his letters. She read on for some time, and then she began to feel chilly, and looking up she saw that the fire was getting low.

'I'll go down to the study,' she thought. 'There's sure to be a good fire there.'

As she went down-stairs it struck her that she would take a look into the schoolroom, and just notice if the 'post-office' drawers were shut, and all looking as usual.

'I might even,' she said to herself, 'count the stamps and compare my counting with Leo's to-morrow.'

But it was dark in the schoolroom. The fire, however, was not quite out; she turned to look for a match or a spill to light one of the candles. Her back was turned to the door, but as she stood there she heard it creak a little as some one pushed it open and came into the room. And this some one, much to her surprise, marched straight up to the stamp drawer, not to the money one, as if well acquainted with the arrangements, and by the light which came in from the hall stood quietly helping himself to some stamps. And who do you think it was? Why no one in the world but Leo's father himself!

Mamma all but burst out laughing, but she managed to stay quite still for a moment. Then she called out: 'What *are* you doing in that drawer?'

It was papa's turn to jump then! But he soon got over his start.

'What are you doing there all by yourself in the dark?' he said. 'And what should I be doing but taking a stamp or two, of course,' he went on, coolly. 'I've always forgotten to say what a good idea it is to have stamps and wrappers and things so handy here. I never knew you kept them here till a few nights ago, when I came in here to see if there was any coal, as my fire was nearly out, and the drawer was open.'

'Ah,' thought Mamma, 'Leo did say he had asked Cynthia to shut it the night he had a headache, and no doubt she forgot.'

'And,' papa went on, 'I was so glad to see where the stamps were, as I sometimes run short. Since then I've helped myself to whatever I wanted, two or three times.'

The Culprit

'So *you* are the culprit,' Leo's mother exclaimed, laughing. And then she told the whole story.

His father was very much interested, and very sorry to have caused any anxiety. He put a whole shilling into the 'till,' which more than put Leo's accounts straight. And the next day he did something still nicer. He brought Leo home the neatest little letter-weigher you ever saw, and told him to add a new rule, to say that letters should be weighed at a charge of a farthing each, in case anyone was in doubt how many stamps to put on. And he also gave Leo a present of a packet of big envelopes of different sizes, which he told him he might sell for a halfpenny each, as they were thick and strong. So Leo's business is flourishing and increasing very much, and he has even thoughts of adding luggage labels and registered-letter envelopes to his stock in trade.

And since the night that mamma watched for the burglars, not a single stamp or postcard or anything has ever been missing.

DENIS IS FRIGHTENED. PAGE 121.

BRAVE LITTLE DENIS.

The brave man is not he who feels no fear,

For that were stupid and irrational;

But he whose noble soul its fear subdues,

And bravely dares the danger nature shrinks from.

JOANNA BAILLIE.

CHAPTER I.—WHAT IS 'BRAVE?'

 The news had come up to the nursery, and there was great excitement and rejoicing. Linda and Nettie chattered so fast, and had so many questions to ask, that the 'big' boys, Alex and Lambert, when they came in to tea could not at first find out what it was all about, or get anyone to explain. And when at last baby—Miss Baby, who was two years old and quite understood that, when nurse wanted to speak, it was not the time to pull her shoes off and complain that 'hers toes was told'—condescended to be quiet and let poor nurse answer, the noise did not grow any less, I can assure you.

'Going to Baronscourt for Christmas. Hurrah!' shouted Alex. 'Three cheers for Granny, Lambert,' which Lambert was only too ready to join in.

'Do you think Granny will make us a Christmas-tree, nurse?' asked Nettie.

'She *should*,' said Linda, 'because of missing last year, you know.'

'Me kismas-tee, too,' said Baby.

'Silly little girl, everybody can't have a Christmas-tree for themselves,' said Linda; at which snub Baby began her preparations for a scream, which was only averted by Alex good-naturedly picking up his little sister and instructing her to give three cheers for Granny.

'Now join too, Denis,' said Linda. 'Why don't you cheer too?'

Denis raised his grave little face.

'I want to finish this story,' he said, dropping his eyes again on the book in his hands.

'What a fancy he's taken for reading, all of a sudden,' said Linda in a lower voice to nurse. 'I don't believe he understands it. He reads awfully slowly when he's at his lessons.'

'Well, Miss Linda, he's only five,' said nurse. 'It's nice for him to find something to keep him quiet sometimes. But he is rather strange this afternoon. I don't know what he's got in his head, sitting there by himself, though to be sure he's always a good bit quieter than his brothers.'

'He's such a baby for his age,' said Linda, rather contemptuously. 'When Alex was seven—that's only two years older than Denis is now—he could do all sorts of things—jump his pony and play cricket, and'——

'I don't think you can remember much about it, Linda,' said Alex, who had overheard her. 'When I was seven you were only five, and that's three years ago, and when Lam was five he couldn't do any better than Den.'

'Because Lambert was delicate, and Denis is not a bit delicate; he's just very babyish,' said Linda, turning away, as if that settled the question.

Denis looked up and opened his lips as if going to speak, but then shut them again and said nothing.

'Aren't you glad to go to Baronscourt, Den?' said gentle little Nettie, the sister who came next him in age. She was sitting beside him at the tea-table, and spoke in rather a low voice. 'Don't you remember how pretty it is there? It's only six months since we were there last. You can't have forgotten it.'

'No,' said Denis; 'I've not forgotten it.'

'Then, aren't you glad to go?'

'I'm glad to see Granny and Prince,' said Denis; but that was all Nettie could get out of him.

He was always a quiet little boy, but during the next few days, if anyone had noticed him closely, it would have been seen that he was even quieter than usual. But these next few days were very busy ones, for the Christmas visit to Baronscourt had been decided on hurriedly, and the nursery arrangements were rather upset. Only once, when the children's mother had come up to see them, she noticed Denis sitting silently in a corner with a very grave look on his little face.

'Is he not well?' she asked nurse, and nurse, after a glance in the child's direction, replied 'that she did not think he was ill; he was often very quiet—it would pass off again.'

'The change to Baronscourt will brighten him up,' said his mother. And then she went on to tell nurse some of the arrangements.

'I had a letter this morning,' she said. 'The house will be very full, but they can take us all in. The girls will have the little room next to mine, and the boys will have the turret room at the end of the picture gallery.'

A movement beside her made her stop and look round. Denis had left his corner and was standing beside her, listening with all his ears, and gazing up in her face with his large soft blue eyes.

37

'And where will nurse, and 'Liza, and baby, and me sleep,' he asked.

His mother laughed.

'You won't be forgotten,' she said. 'Nurse and baby will have the old nursery, and you will have a little cot beside them, I daresay.'

A look of satisfaction crept over his face.

'And 'Liza?' he asked.

'Oh, poor 'Liza won't be forgotten either,' said his mother.

Denis grew brighter after this conversation, and at tea that afternoon, when all the children were talking, he joined in as usual.

'Mother told me where you'se all to sleep at Granny's house,' he announced, impatiently. 'I'm to sleep with nurse and baby.'

'Yes, of course, because you're such a baby yourself,' said Linda. 'Nettie and I are to have a room to ourselves like we have at home. I hope it'll be the turret room at the end of the gallery. I do so love the gallery—at night, you know, when the moon comes in through the coloured glass and makes all the faces of the pictures look so queer—red and purple, and blue and green. The red ones look quite jolly, but the green and blue ones look dreadful.'

'Like ghosts,' suggested Lambert.

'Yes, something like that, I suppose,' said Linda, as if she was in the habit of seeing ghosts, and knew quite what they were like.

'Or like us when we play snapdragon—at the end, you know, when they throw salt in among the brandy,' suggested Nettie.

'Don't talk about that, please, Nettie,' whispered Denis, tugging softly at his sister's arm.

Nettie looked surprised, but she understood Den better than did any of the others, so she said no more; but later in the evening, when they were alone, she asked him what he meant.

'I don't know,' said Denis; 'don't ask me; I want to forget about it,' and he gave a little shiver.

And question as Nettie would, he could not be got to explain further.

There was only one Sunday at home before the day came for going. It was a cold and snowy day; too cold, it was decided, for the children to go to church, so in the afternoon their mother sent for them all to read with her. The stormy weather led to their talking about adventures in winter—about poor travellers being lost in the snow, and the brave things that had been done to rescue them sometimes, and the children's mother told them some stories which they thought very interesting.

'What is "brave?"' asked Denis suddenly. He was sitting beside his mother, and was holding her hand.

Mother looked round.

'Suppose you each answer Denis's question?' she said. 'I'll begin with you, Alex, as you're the oldest. What does true bravery mean?'

'Den didn't say "true" bravery, mother,' objected Linda, who had already shrugged her plump shoulders contemptuously at her little brother's question, with a muttered 'So silly—anybody could tell that.'—'He only said, "what does 'brave' mean?" If you say "true bravery," it gets more puzzling.'

Mother looked at Linda with a rather amused expression.

'That is why I added the word you object to, my dear Linda. I *want* you all to think about it a little, not just to answer what "anybody can tell," without reflecting at all.' Linda blushed. *Sometimes* it was annoying that mother had such quick ears. But she said nothing. 'Come, Alex,' continued mother, 'what is true bravery?'

'Oh, I don't know. *I* don't see anything puzzling,' said Alex, looking puzzled, nevertheless. 'It just means not being afraid of anything. It's just the way people are made. Some are afraid, and some aren't. I'm never afraid, but it's just that I'm made that way,' he went on.

'But if that's it, it has nothing to do with being good,' said Lambert, who was more thoughtful than Alex. 'I mean, it's no use thinking about a thing that comes of itself like that, mother. And yet being brave is always counted as if it was something good, something to be praised for.'

He raised his face to his mother's, questioningly.

'Well, try and put your feeling about it into words,' she said.

Lambert hesitated.

'I know,' said Linda, confidently. 'Mother means that true bravery is when there's no pretending about it. Some people who are really afraid *pretend* they're not—boastingly, you know.'

'And that is *one* sort of cowardice,' said her mother. 'They don't own the truth, because they're afraid of being thought afraid. You're right so far, Linda; but you do not go quite far enough.'

A little eager sound from Nettie caught her attention.

'Well, Nettie, have you something to say?' she asked.

'I don't quite know,' Nettie began. 'I thought I could see it, but I'm not sure. But isn't it a little like this, mother—that whether one's afraid or not, one should try to do anything that's right to do?'

Her mother smiled.

'Yes, that is something like it,' she said. 'That's what I have been wanting you to get to see. The *mastering the fear*—that is the truest bravery of all. Not for what others may or may not think of us, but because it is right. When a duty comes in the way, something right or good or kind to do, a really brave person, man, woman, or child, will do it even if it is something which they fear to do.'

'But still,' Lambert objected, 'there are some people praised for being brave who don't feel fear—like what Alex said. Should they not be praised, mother?'

'Certainly they should be praised for doing right at risk to themselves,' said his mother. 'It is a great blessing to be naturally brave—what is called physically brave. But I doubt if even the naturally bravest men have never known fear. It is the determination to do their duty at all costs that keeps them brave and gives strength and courage. And this even the most timid by nature can learn; so this is what I call true bravery. Not the unreasoning courage of a lion or a bulldog, but the courage of a man who knows his duty and will do it.'

The children sat silent—each in his or her own way thinking over their mother's words. One only had said nothing, but he was pondering deeply, and his mother, glancing round, saw Denis gazing before him with a curious look in his innocent blue eyes.

'Do you understand a little, Denis, my boy?' she asked, with a smile.

'I fink so,' he answered softly, and she felt him squeeze the hand he held. But that was all he said.

CHAPTER II.—GRANNY AND THE CHILDREN.

Two days later, in the dusk of a mid-winter afternoon, they were all arriving at Baronscourt. The ground was white with snow.

'What a storm there must have been here,' said the children's father. 'The snow is quite deep, much deeper than with us.' For their home was at some hours' distance, and farther south.

'Do you fink anybody will be lost in the snow, Nettie?' whispered Denis to his sister.

They two were seated opposite their father and mother in their grandmother's brougham, which had been sent to the station to meet them, with a large covered wagonette for the rest of the party.

Nettie smiled at Denis.

'Not here, Den,' she said. 'It's very seldom people are lost in the snow in England. It's in far-away hilly countries like Switzerland.'

'Was it there that mother was reading about?' asked Denis, only half satisfied.

'Yes,' said Nettie. 'It's there that they have the great big dogs that are so good, going looking for the poor people in the snow.'

'I shouldn't like to live in that country, though I *would* love the dogs,' said Denis. And then jumping up in his seat with a scream of delight, 'O Nettie, O Nettie,' he cried, 'look, look! There's dear little Prin coming to meet us all in the snow; dear little Prin; oh, I hope he won't get covered up. Mayn't we stop to take him in?'

'We're quite close to the house, dear,' said his mother, smiling at his pleasure. 'Prin will be all right. Granny will not let him go far alone, you may be sure.'

And as she said so, Prince, whose little smooth, jet-black body looked very funny in the snow, turned round after two or three sharp barks of welcome, and made for the house again.

'He's gone to tell them we're come,' said Denis; 'isn't he a *sensible* dog, Nettie? I don't think I love *anybody* better than Prin,' he said, ecstatically.

41

They were at the front door by this time, and there, a little way back in the shelter of the hall, for it was very cold, and she was no longer a young lady, stood dear Granny waiting to welcome them.

Granny, I must tell you, was not the children's grandmother, but the great-aunt of their mother. She seemed, therefore, a kind of great-grandmother to Denis and his brothers and sisters, and to have called her 'Aunt,' or anything else but 'Granny,' would have been impossible. She was old; very old, I daresay she seemed to the children, but yet there was a delightful sort of youngness about her, which made them feel as if they could tell her anything, with a certainty of being understood. And of all the children she loved and who loved her, I don't think any felt this beautiful sort of sympathy more than quiet little Denis. It was a long time—in child life a very long time—since he had seen her, six months ago, a tenth part of the whole time which Denis had spent in this world—but when he saw dear Granny standing there in the doorway, her sweet gentle old face all over smiles of pleasure, it seemed to him that he had never been away from her at all.

'Dear Granny,' he said softly, when his turn came to be kissed, 'dear Granny, I do 'amember you so well—you and Prin;' and he was not at all offended when the others laughed at his funny little speech—a long speech for Den; he thought they were only laughing because they all felt so pleased to be back with Granny and Prin again.

'My dear little boy,' Granny said, as she kissed him, 'this is very sweet of you. And you may be sure Granny and Prin haven't forgotten you.'

And Denis, looking up, thought that Granny was the prettiest lady in the world, 'next to mother.' She *was* very pretty, at least in the sight of those who do not think beauty is only to be found in the bright eyes and fresh roses of youth. And, indeed, Granny's eyes were bright still, and when she was very pleased, or sometimes when she was very vexed—for Granny could be vexed when it was right she should be—her cheeks, soft and withered as they were, would grow rosy as when she was a girl. They were rosy just now, with pleasure, of course, and perhaps with a little tiredness; for there were a great many people staying in the house, and large as Granny's heart was, it was rather tiring to so old a lady to attend to so many guests.

'I am so glad you have come, my dear,' she whispered to Denis's mother. 'You will help me better than anyone. It was right I think to fill the old house again this Christmas, but my heart fails me sometimes when I think of those who are no longer among us. And yet they *are* among us—just at these times, my dear, all the old faces seem to be smiling back at me, the last of the generation. The house seems filled with their presence to me as much as with the living friends who are about me.'

The children's mother pressed Granny's arm.

'Dear Granny,' she said, 'don't talk like that. We couldn't do without you yet awhile. You are tired, dear Granny. Now it will be all right. I shall do all, and you must rest.'

Denis had been standing close beside them. He heard what Granny said without understanding thoroughly what she meant, and a very grave, awe-struck look came over his face.

'Does Granny mean that they come out really?' he said to himself with a little shiver. 'Granny doesn't seem frightened,' he added. 'I mustn't be frightened, but I'm so glad I'm to sleep in nurse's room.'

Poor little man. There was disappointment in store for him. His mother would not let Granny go up-stairs to show them their rooms as she wished to do.

'No, no, Granny,' she said, 'I know them all quite well. Take Granny back to the library, Edith,' she added to one of the young ladies staying in the house. 'I'll come down in five minutes when I have settled the children in the nursery.'

Granny's maid met them at the top of the first stair, and went with them to their rooms.

'Yes,' said the children's mother, 'that will all do beautifully. Linda and Nettie in the room beside me, nurse and baby in the old nursery, the boys in one of the turret rooms, and Denis—let me see—isn't there to be a little bed for him in the nursery?'

They were on their way from the nursery to the boys' room when she said this; Denis beside his mother still, holding her hand.

'No, ma'am,' said Tanner, the maid, 'my lady thought Master Denis would be better in the little room beside his brothers'. It's a very little room, but big enough, I daresay, for such a little gentleman. It would not have been easy to put another bed in the nursery, without filling it up so. And my lady thought Master Denis would be proud to have a room of his own.'

'Yes, indeed,' said his mother; 'how kind of her.'

They were passing along the picture gallery. All of them together, except nurse and baby, who had stayed behind by the nursery fire. Linda, Alex, Lambert, and Nettie in front; mother and Denis and Tanner behind. Denis tightened his hold of his mother's hand, but said nothing.

'I wish *we* had one of the turret rooms,' said Linda; 'this gallery is *so* lovely to run along every time one goes to one's room. I like this gallery the best of anything in the house.'

'And best of all in the moonlight,' said Alex. 'Don't you remember, Linda? For my part I prefer it in the day-time, or well lit up, like just now.'

'What a goose you are!' said Linda. 'Do you mean to say you'd be *afraid* to come here in the moonlight?'

'Hush, children, don't talk so foolishly,' said their mother, for she never liked that silly kind of talk, especially before the little ones. 'I quite agree with you, Linda, about this gallery being charming.'

They all stood for a moment—they were close to the end door by now, the door that opened into the anteroom, from whence opened the turret rooms— and looked back. It was worth looking at. Lighted by the old-fashioned lamps that hung at intervals from the dark oak ceiling, which reflected their rays like a black mirror, the old gallery, with its coloured glass windows at one side, the small, leadened panes looking quaint and mysterious, though their tints could not, of course, be seen, and the rows and rows of silent portraits looking down upon you from the other side, seemed like a dream of a long-ago world, the merry voices and bright glances of the children striking one as almost out of place, and the grave faces appearing to gaze at them in disapproval.

'It was not meant for a picture gallery long ago,' said their mother: 'if it had been, these windows would not have been placed so, and they certainly would not have had coloured glass. These portraits used to be in the large saloon and the drawing-room, but they made them look so gloomy that Granny's father hung them up here,' and so saying she opened the door and crossed the passage to the boys' room, followed by all the five.

'How jolly!' said Alex and Lambert in a breath, and with good reason, for their room looked the picture of comfort, with its deep window-seats and wainscoted walls, and the radiance of the brightly-burning fire over all.

'The boys don't have fires in their bedroom at home,' observed Linda.

'And they need not have one here every day,' said their mother. 'It's just for a welcome at the beginning.'

'And because it really is so cold. I hardly think my lady would be pleased if they hadn't one,' said Tanner with a smile, which made Alex and Lambert think she was very kind indeed.

Then they all turned to look at Denis's little room. It was very snug and cosy, though very tiny. It did not open into his brothers', but was just across the little anteroom.

'You will be very happy in here, won't you, Den?' said his mother brightly;

and not noticing that the little fellow did not reply, she hurried away, for she was anxious to go down to the library and help Granny with afternoon tea for her guests.

CHAPTER III.—THE PICTURE GALLERY.

 Linda and Nettie turned to go back to the nursery, where tea was waiting for them. Denis took hold of Nettie's hand to go too, but Alex and Lambert remained behind to explore further their new quarters.

'Nettie,' said Denis, pulling his little sister back a little. 'I wish I might have slept in the old nursery with nurse and baby.'

'Why, Denis dear?' said Nettie in surprise; 'your little room is so pretty, and I never knew you were frightened of sleeping alone.'

'I'm not,' said Denis. 'It's not that.'

'What is it, then?' said Nettie. 'It's such a pity you don't like it, when Granny's planned it so to please us. We should seem pleased, Denis, for you know Granny is rather sad. Last Christmas she was too sad to have anybody, for poor old uncle had died, you know. And it's *so* good of her to have us all this Christmas. Mother says Granny's only pleasure is to make other people happy.'

'I do love Granny,' said Denis.

'Well then, don't you think you should try to be pleased with what she's planned for us—with your nice little room?'

'I *are* pleased with my room,' replied Denis. 'I like it werry much.'

Nettie stared at him as if she thought he was losing his senses.

'Then what *do* you mean?' she asked.

Denis looked round. They were still in the picture gallery. He pulled Nettie on, and when they were in the passage on to which at this end the gallery opened, he shut the door and drew his sister into a corner.

'Nettie,' he said, 'you won't never tell, will you?'

'No,' said Nettie, rather rashly.

'I wouldn't tell anybody but you, Nettie. Linda can't hear, can she?'

'Oh no, she's run on to the nursery.'

'Nettie,' he continued, 'it's not my room. It's the picshurs,' here he shook his head solemnly. 'It's having to pass the picshurs. It's dreadful. But, O

Nettie, don't tell. It began last year when we was here. They try to catch me, Nettie. I'm almost sure they do. They come down off the wall and run after me—at least I *fink* they do.'

'But they *can't*,' said Nettie, very much impressed, but still full of common sense; 'they *can't*, Denis. Pictures is pictures—they can't walk or run. Just think, they're not alive—they're not even like dolls. They're only thin bits of paper or wood—or—or—whatever it is pictures are painted on.'

But Denis still shook his head.

'I know that,' he said. 'I've thought of that, but it's no good. When I'm not there I think that way, but as soon as I'm there it begins. Their eyes all look at me, and I'm sure they begin to get down to run after me as soon as I've passed. It's worst at night, like now, when the lamps is lighted. It isn't so bad in the day. But, O Nettie, it must be worstest in the moonlight,' and he gave a little shiver; 'don't you 'amember what Linda said about it—all the colours on the faces, you know?'

'But anyway,' said practical Nettie, 'you don't need to see them in the moonlight. You never need to go along there after the lamps are put out at night.'

'No,' said Denis, but not as if he found much consolation in the thought.

'And if you'd let me tell mother,' continued Nettie, 'I'm sure she'd change it some way. You might sleep with Alex, and Lam have your room.'

'*That* wouldn't do any good,' objected Denis. 'It's not the room I mind.'

'Oh no, of course. I forgot. But Den, I daresay it could be settled for you to sleep in the old nursery after all.'

'No,' said Denis. 'I'm going to try, Nettie. I want to be brave, and I don't want to vex Granny and mother. So you mustn't tell. You won't, I know, 'cos you've p'omised. I'm going to try running very fast along the gallery every time and look at the window side, not at the pictures. Then *p'raps* it won't come.'

'It. What?' asked Nettie, in an awe-struck tone. She was very much impressed by the whole, and felt no small admiration for Denis. 'Is there one more than the others that tries to catch you?'

'No,' said Denis. 'I mean the *feeling* when I say "it." Oh, it's dreadful!' he repeated. 'But do you know, Nettie,' he went on, 'I fink Granny knows somefin about it. She said somefin to mother. But *she* didn't seem frightened. P'raps they don't try to catch her. She said they smiled at her?' and Denis looked up at Nettie with great bewilderment.

'She couldn't have meant the pictures,' said Nettie decisively.

'She said, the old faces, and there isn't any other old faces,' persisted Denis.

'Well, never mind about that,' said Nettie, resolving privately, nevertheless, to try to find out what it was Granny *had* said. 'You didn't understand, perhaps, Denis. You're only a very little boy still, you know, and big people do say things sometimes that sound quite different from what they mean. We must go to the nursery to tea now, but I'll tell you one thing. Every time you have to run along the gallery I'll *try* to go with you, and then p'raps you'll get not to mind. Of course if you were frightened in the night, you have Alex and Lambert close to.'

'I'm not frightened in the night. I'm not frightened *nowhere* 'cept *there*. Thank you, dear Nettie. You'll hold my hand, won't you? and we'll run together, and p'raps I'll get not to mind. I don't fink I can leave off minding, but I want to be brave.'

And holding up his little face to be kissed, Denis went back to the nursery with Nettie, his heart somewhat lighter, I think, for having confided his secret to some one.

It did not occur to Nettie that it would have been right for her to tell it. For one thing she had 'promised,' and with these children that word was a solemn one. Then, too, she fully shared Denis's dislike to complain or give trouble, partly from the wish to please Granny who was 'so kind,' partly from the strange reserve one often finds in even very little children. Few but those who have watched them very constantly and closely have any idea how much children will endure rather than complain.

For some time nothing happened to cause Nettie to think more seriously of poor little Den's strange fancy. He seemed to wish not to speak of it, and she did not lead him to do so, hoping always that he might come to forget it. But she did not forget her other promise. Every time that Denis had to traverse the dreaded gallery, his faithful little sister, if she knew of it, was sure to start up to go with him. They used to run as fast as the slippery polished floor would allow them, holding each other's hands, and, Denis at least, steadily avoiding to look at the portraits. In the morning early he did not mind it so much, though even then Nettie often came to fetch him, if he had not already made his appearance when Linda and she were summoned to the nursery breakfast.

'It's queer how Miss Nettie and Master Denis cling to each other,' the under-nurse remarked one day. 'I never noticed it so much before. It's like as if he couldn't move without her.'

'Miss Nettie's a very kind little girl,' the head-nurse replied, 'but I do think she spoils Master Denis a little. He's getting a big boy.'

That very evening, as they were beginning tea—and tea-time at Christmas is always after dark—nurse told Denis to run to his brothers' room to tell them to come, for Alex and Lambert, having gone off to wash their hands, had not returned. Denis began slowly to clamber down from his chair, somewhat encumbered by Prince, who was, as usual, in his arms.

'Make haste, Master Denis,' said nurse, rather sharply, though not unkindly. 'You shouldn't have the dog always in your arms, my dear. At meal times it isn't nice.'

Denis cast an appealing glance at Nettie. She had already left her place and was at his side.

'Put Prince down, Den,' she said, and the little boy did so, while Prince, shaking himself, ran to the hearth-rug, moving round and round till he had burrowed an imaginary hole, where he comfortably ensconced himself.

'Mayn't I go instead of Denis?' said Nettie. 'I'd run much quicker.'

Another time nurse would probably have said 'yes,' but her attention was aroused. She did not quite understand Denis and Nettie, and it seemed to her that they were not just the same as usual.

'No, my dear,' she said. 'It is better for Master Denis to go, as I told him first.'

But the children hesitated.

'Mayn't we both go?' persisted Nettie, taking Denis's hand. But nurse shook her head.

'Miss Nettie, Master Denis will never be a big, sensible boy if you treat him so. Why should he not run off himself at once when I tell him?'

The tears came to Nettie's eyes, but Denis gave her hand a little squeeze. 'Whatever you do, don't tell,' the squeeze seemed to say, and Nettie dared not do anything more.

'I'll go, Nettie dear,' said Denis, and his little sister, looking at him, saw that, though he was very pale, there was a look of determination on his face. He turned to the door, and Nettie, choking back a sob, turned back to her place at table, when suddenly the door burst open with a bang, and the two truants, Alex and Lambert, rushed in breathless and laughing. With a great sigh of relief Denis clambered up again on to his chair.

'We've had such a race,' Alex began; 'we wanted to see who'd get to the

49

end of the gallery first. I expect those old grandfathers and grandmothers are rather shocked at the noise we make, sometimes.'

'There's one at this end who does look so cross,' said Lambert. 'The one with the yellow satin dress, and her mouth screwed up *so*.' He illustrated his words with great effect—'just like Linda, when she's in a temper. Ah! yes, that's it, Linda,' for his sister had turned from him with dignified disgust. 'I'm sure I don't want such an ugly old thing for a great-grandmother, but I'm afraid she must be some relation, she's so like Linda.'

'Nurse,' began Linda, '*do* make Lambert leave off, he is *so*'——

But a voice at the door interrupted her.

'Boys,' it said, and the children looking round caught sight of their father. Up jumped the boys, and would have rushed towards him, had he not stopped them. 'Don't be so excited,' he went on. 'I only want to tell you that if the weather continues as it is, your cousins and I are going to Hatchetts to skate to-morrow. There is to be a large party there, for it is a capital place. Alex and Lambert, you may come with us if you like. We shall be back before your bedtime, any way.'

There was a shout of satisfaction from the boys, but Linda looked considerably annoyed.

'I'm sure father wouldn't take you,' she whispered to Lambert, who was sitting beside her, 'if he knew how rude you are.'

'I wish Nettie and I might go,' she said aloud. '*Couldn't* we, father? The pond here is such a horrid little place for skating, and we can skate so well now.'

'Me go too. Mayn't me go too?' began Baby, at which everybody except Linda laughed.

'You, my pet!' said her father. 'Why, you'd be lost in the snow, and what would we do then without our Baby?'

Denis looked very grave.

'Prin would try to get her out,' he remarked. 'Like the dogs up in those snowy hills.'

'He means the St Bernard dogs,' said Nettie. 'Mother told us stories about them.'

'Ah, yes!' said her father. 'But they are ever so much bigger than Prince, my boy. Much more fear of Prince being lost himself in a snowstorm, than of his rescuing anyone else, poor little dog.'

'But there isn't going to be a snowstorm,' said Linda. 'Father, mightn't we go—I anyway?'

'No, my dear,' said her father. 'It's too uncertain. I hope the weather will keep up. If it doesn't, no one can go. But it is too uncertain for little girls: the boys must learn to rough it, but you and Nettie must be content to skate on the pond here for the present.'

Linda's face clouded over still more. She hated being called 'a little girl,' especially before her brothers. Her father turned away, either not seeing, or not wishing to seem to see, her vexation.

'Get to bed early, then, and be up in good time,' he called out to the boys as he left the room.

CHAPTER IV.—MASTERING THE FEAR.

 The morning dawned bright and clear. The frost seemed settled, the sky gave no signs of storm. The party of gentlemen and boys started on their skating expedition in great spirits.

'Do you wish you were big enough to go too, Denis?' said Nettie, as they stood at the door after watching them start.

'Not without Prinnie,' said Denis, hugging his pet, as he spoke. 'I don't care to go anywhere without Prin, and it would hurt his dear little feet to put skates on them, wouldn't it.'

Nettie burst out laughing at the idea.

'Come in, children. Don't stay there in the cold,' their mother called out; and as they went into the library at her summons, Granny asked them what they were laughing at.

"Twas Nettie,' said Denis, gravely as usual; and when Nettie told her what had amused her, Granny looked rather anxiously at Denis.

'And do you never laugh, my boy?' she asked. 'If you say funny things that make other people laugh, how is it you don't laugh yourself?'

Denis lifted up his face for a kiss, but there was an expression in his eyes which Granny did not quite understand.

'That child looks—I don't know how exactly,' she said to his mother, when Denis and Nettie had gone up-stairs. 'He is such a dear little fellow, but there is a look of suffering or endurance in his face that I can't understand. Your nurses are really kind to the children, I suppose?'

'Perfectly—I'm sure of it,' replied Denis's mother. 'He is always quiet. Perhaps he is a little disappointed to-day at seeing Alex and Lambert go off.'

But Granny wasn't satisfied. She resolved to watch little Denis for herself.

He was looking graver than usual even, for the thought was heavy on his mind that with his brothers away the whole day, the dreaded gallery would be worse than ever. With Alex or Lambert at hand, he could often manage to make the journeys to and from the nursery in their company; but to-day he had no one to depend on but Nettie, and nurse did not like Nettie always roaming about with him. It would not do to get Nettie scolded for being so

52

good to him. Poor Denis! He felt terribly deserted as he followed Nettie upstairs, Prin at his feet.

'Dear Prin,' he whispered, 'I wish it was time for us to go back home where there's no picshur gallery to frighten us. Only then, dear Prin, you wouldn't be coming too, for your home is here, you know, dear Prin.'

Prin wagged his tail and looked up at Denis. It was all that he could do, poor little dog.

The day kept up fine and bright till towards two o'clock. The clouds began to gather in leaden masses, and the dull, gray-blue look one knows so well in winter, came over the sky.

'I'm afraid it's going to snow again,' said the children's mother, on their way home from the despised pond, where Linda and Nettie and some of the young ladies staying in the house had been amusing themselves by skating, and Denis had been allowed to slide, with Prince at his heels, of course.

'What a nuisance!' said one of the girls. 'All our skating will be over if it does, till the pond is cleared again. It is just nice now. And oh, by the bye, you will be uneasy about uncle and the boys if it snows'—for this young lady was a cousin of Linda's and the others—'won't you, aunt? Hatchetts is an awkward place to get away from in a snowstorm.'

Denis listened with all his ears, while his mother looked up anxiously at the sky.

'If it really comes on as bad as that, I hope they won't attempt to come home to-night,' she said.

'They might be losted in the snow, and we have no big dogs!' exclaimed Denis in great distress, as already a few flakes began to fall.

'Don't be afraid, my boy,' said his mother. 'Father will not do anything rash, you may be sure.'

But her relief nevertheless was great when, about four o'clock, a servant who had started with the party in the morning, came back with the news that the gentlemen were going to stay away all night. He had started as soon as the weather gave signs of changing, so he had got back without difficulty. The snow had not begun yet where they were skating, he said, but it was plain to be seen that it was coming, though the gentlemen hoped to have two or three hours' good exercise, as they would dine and sleep with the friend on whose property they were.

It was well they had so decided. By five o'clock the snowstorm was at its height. It was too dark to distinguish anything from the windows, but news came in from outside that the snow lay deep already, and gave no signs of leaving off.

'We must make ourselves as comfortable as we can,' said Granny, as she told the servants to put more wood on the fire, 'and be thankful that our dear ones are not out in any danger. So you've come to say good-night, dears, have you?' she went on, as the little girls and Denis just then came into the drawing-room. 'Good-night, my darlings; you've had a happy day, I hope, in spite of the weather?'

'Oh yes, Granny,' they answered eagerly. 'We've had blind-man's buff with Cousin Edith and the others in the hall.'

'And now you're sleepy and ready for bed. Good-night and pleasant dreams,' and the children trotted off again. Granny had kissed Denis among the others, and had been pleased to see his little face rosier than usual, thanks to the romp they had been having. Afterwards she wondered to herself for not having remembered that with his brothers away the little fellow would be rather lonely in his part of the house, but somehow it did not come into her mind just then. Nor did it occur to his mother. So the children were put to bed as usual, and Denis made no complaint. Indeed, once in his little room he felt quite safe. Nurse had brought him herself through the gallery well wrapped up in her arms, having undressed him by the nursery fire, and he hid his face on her shoulder as she carried him, and avoided all sight of his silent enemies on the wall.

'You're quite comfortable, Master Denis?' she asked, as she left him.

'Quite,' he replied, 'and nurse, you'll let me have Prin up to-morrow morning?'

'Oh yes, dear,' she answered kindly; 'you were a good little boy about him this afternoon. You shall have him to-morrow.'

Denis gave a sigh as he composed himself to sleep. He was not quite easy in his mind about Prince, whom nurse had sent downstairs because Baby was in a cross humour, and cried when he jumped on her.

'Poor Prince,' thought Denis. 'I hope he's not very unhappy. Robert' (Robert was a young footman) 'p'omised to be kind to him, and not let him go out in the snow. I hope father, and Alex, and Lambert won't be lost in the snow, 'cos Prin is too little to get them out. I hope'—— But what he hoped more was lost in a confusion of ideas—Prince, and his father and brothers, and the falling snow seemed all mixed together in his brain, for Denis fell fast asleep.

The snowstorm was over, though he did not know it; since six or seven

54

o'clock no more had fallen. The clouds dispersed, though some of them were still to be seen hurry-scurrying over the face of the moon in a very provoking way, for she had come out in full, anxious to see what was going on down there on the earth, which she had not had a good sight of for some time past. She peeped in at the window of little Denis's room and saw him sleeping sweetly, his little face flushed as he lay, a contrast to those of the long rows of Granny's faded ancestors which she glanced at for a moment, through the windows of the gallery, as the clouds passed by.

Suddenly Denis woke, and half-started up in his bed. What had awakened him? For a minute or two he could not tell. It was not the moon, though she was there again, peeping in at the chinks left at the corners of the window-blind, and lighting up the white cover of his bed. No, it could not have been the moon, for, as he became more fully awake, he felt sure he had heard some sound. He sat up and listened. Yes, there it was again, a low wail or cry, once or twice repeated, and seeming not far off. Denis sat bolt upright; he did not feel afraid, he only wondered very much what it could be; again he heard it; it sounded like a cry for help. What could it be? Visions of Alex and Lambert in the snow came into his mind. How dreadful if it was one of them! and the cry sounded so near too, as if it were some one at the side door to the garden—a door which opened close by the stair leading to the nursery. What could he do? Oh, if he only had one of these great brave dogs that his mother had read about! The thought made him start—was not the cry like the whine of a dog. Could it be Prince, his own dear little Prince out there alone; poor tender Prince, that could not bear the cold, and would be frightened? Could Robert have forgotten him? Up jumped Denis, and without stopping for slippers or dressing-gown ran to the door.

'I will call Alex and Lambert,' he thought; 'they'll come with me to let in poor Prin.'

But suddenly he remembered that Alex and Lambert were not there; they were staying away till to-morrow. Denis stopped short—he must go *alone* to rescue Prince, alone through the terrible gallery. Bad enough in the daytime and with Nettie's hand, or in the evening with all the cheerful lamps lighted, what would it be in the middle of the night, in the dark?—no, not in the dark, as just then his eyes fell on the strip of brightness across the floor; worse still, it would be moonlight in the gallery, and Denis shivered as he remembered what Linda had said of the look of the old portraits in the moonlight.

'No,' he said aloud, 'I can't go. I can't, poor little Prin. I can't pass along there and feel them running after me with their faces all red and blue and green, and dreadful. I can't.'

But just then a rather low piteous whine reached his ears. It half broke his heart to hear it, and at the same moment, as if by magic, some of his mother's words that Sunday afternoon returned to the little fellow's mind. 'Mastering the fear—that is the truest bravery of all; when something good or kind to do comes in the way, to do it even if one is frightened.' Denis stood up again. 'I'll try to be brave,' he thought. 'I fink God will take care of me if I go to let Prin in, so that he won't die of cold.'

CHAPTER V.—A FRIGHT AND ITS CONSEQUENCES.

He drew on his little dressing-gown, for he was shivering with cold and excitement. But his slippers he would not put on. 'I can run so much faster without them,' he said, speaking to himself in a low voice. Then he opened the door, crossed the little anteroom, and hesitating a moment, threw open the large door of the gallery. An instant he waited before he found courage to look up. Then he did so, with a half-acknowledged feeling that if anything *too* appalling met his eye, he could still rush back into the shelter of his own room.

But all was still, strangely still, and the curious effect of the moonlight, streaming in, in fitful patches through the coloured windows, for a moment made him forget his fears in a sort of awe-struck admiration. It was even stranger than Linda had described it, for the clouds quickly rushing across the moon, caused a mixture of light and shadow, coloured by the tints of the glass, like broken and confused rainbows. And had Denis not been too frightened to look at the faces on the wall, the effect of this jumble of light and colour and shadow would have been almost comical.

But a glance was enough. Then literally gathering up his garments—that is to say, taking the skirts of his dressing-gown in his hands—the poor little chap dashed into the enemy's country, looking neither to right nor to left, and ran—his little bare feet making a quick pitter-patter on the polished floor—ran as if for dear life! Fortunately he did not stumble: had he done so, I doubt if he would have been able to get up again—the terrible thought that something had caught him and made him fall would probably have altogether overcome him—but oh how long the gallery seemed, and oh how thankful he was to reach the other end and burst through the swing baize door that closed it!

Here, in the passage, leading to the nursery, all was dark, or seemed so at first, though as Denis felt his way to the staircase, his eyes got used to the darkness, and gradually began to discern some light in it. He knew his way so well that even without this he could have found the stair; and once on it, a little more light came up from the fanlight on the top of the garden-door below, and now Prin's voice was heard again, quite plainly, showing that he was just outside the door, seldom closed to him, poor little dog, as he was accustomed to come in and out by it with the children on their way to and from the garden.

'I'm coming, Prin, dear little Prin,' cried Denis, quite brightly and cheerfully now, as he reached the foot of the stair, and Prin in return gave a hopeful little bark; 'one moment, dear Prin, till Denis opens the door for you,' he went on, as he fumbled for the handle, which he knew he could reach. He reached it, and turned it, but oh, what a disappointment; the door would not open as it did in the daytime—it was bolted! At first Denis thought it might be locked, and he felt about for a key. But there was no key, and peering about in the uncertain light he saw high up something which looked like a bolt—far too high for him to reach, and probably too hard for his little hands to pull back. He had never thought of this, and he was terribly distressed—especially when another faint whine from Prince seemed to ask why he was so slow. But it roused him too.

'Poor Prin,' he said, 'Denis can't get the door open. Den will have to go and get nurse to help. He'll be as quick as he can. Stay there, dear Prin,' and then he turned to climb the stair again, his feet this time perfectly numb with cold. He must get up two flights—past the day-nursery, to where nurse and baby slept, in what was called 'the old nursery,' a story higher than the other. But so long as there was no gallery to face, Denis did not seem to mind. He got on all right till he was crossing the landing or passage on to which the swing-door opened; then just as he was putting his foot on the first step of the second flight he was startled by a noise—a sound of footsteps approaching him, and, oh terror! from the direction of the gallery. In his fear he stood still, as if not knowing what to do. The steps came nearer and nearer with a rather slow, dragging sound. Denis still stood as if turned to stone. The baize door swung open, a light warmer and brighter than the moon rays gleamed through, and a figure stood full in the boy's sight. A tall figure, it seemed to him, clothed in yellow, with pale face and powdered hair, all distinctly seen by the flame of the taper held in its hand.

'The lady in the yellow satin!' screamed poor Denis; 'oh, it's come true! She's got out of the frame to catch me. O mother, mother, it's so dreadful, and I did so try to be brave!'

His eyes closed, his legs gave way, and he half fell forward. What would have happened I don't know, if a sweet, well-known voice had not reached his ears.

'Denis, my boy, don't be frightened. Don't you know me? It's your own old Granny.'

And half-laughing, half-crying, Granny went on talking till the boy took courage again and opened his eyes.

'Granny!' he said, and then shivering again, seemed as if he could hardly believe it.

'Yes, dear, Granny, in her old white cashmere dressing-gown. Look, dear, and see.'

'And white hair, like the picshur,' he said, recovering himself. 'And what a funny thing on the top of your head, Granny—all frilly—like'——

'That's my nightcap,' said Granny, now fairly laughing, and then she went on to explain that from her room, which had an unused door opening on to the same landing as the boys' room, she had heard him moving about, and fearing that something was wrong, and knowing the little fellow to be alone, she had come round by the other way to see.

'For that other door is never opened, and there is a chest of drawers against it,' she said. 'And when I found there was not a little boy in bed in your room, I came back to look for him, you see, Denis, and I thought I heard voices down below. For my ears are sharp still, though I'm such an old woman.'

'It was me talking to poor Prin,' said Denis. And then in his turn he had to explain all, and Granny, taking him back with her to her nice cheerful room where a fire was still burning, rang the bell for her maid, and in a few minutes poor Prince, the cause of all the upset, was happily warming himself and forgetting all his troubles on Granny's hearth-rug.

'I'll go back to bed now, please,' said Denis; 'I'm not a bit frightened now. I don't fink I'll ever be frightened again,' he added in a half-whisper, as he bade Granny a second good-night. And you may fancy how proud he was, when Granny answered, 'Frightened or not, you've shown yourself my own brave little Denis.'

Mother was told all about it next morning, and of the good fruit her words had borne. But as she kissed her little boy, she explained to him and to Nettie, too, that in such a case there would have been no cowardice in telling her of Denis's fears.

'I would not wish any of you to be tried needlessly, dears, you know,' she said. 'It would have been easy to put Denis into another room. Still I am thankful to see that, when there was need, my boy could battle with his fears and master them.'

But somehow, from that time, the picture gallery ceased to be a place of terror to Denis. For one thing, Granny pleased herself by showing him all the old portraits in the bright daytime, and telling him many interesting and curious stories about their originals, till he got to have quite a friendly feeling to the bewigged and bepowdered long-ago ladies and gentlemen. Especially to the lady in the yellow satin dress, with the mouth like Linda's!

Granny often smiled to herself when she put on her old-fashioned lace-frilled nightcap, and thought of how she had frightened poor little Denis. To 'make up,' she said, she gave him a present of Prince to be his very own; and you may be quite sure he was never again left out in the cold and snow, and that no dog ever led a happier life than he, in faithfully serving the brave little master who had overcome his terror, to do a good and kind action.

THE END.